The Goblin Baby

The Goblin Baby

By Berlie Doherty

Illustrated by Lesley Harker

A STEPPING STONE BOOK™
Random House 🏠 New York

For Tim, Verena, and Tommy
—B.D.

Text copyright © 2004 by Berlie Doherty. Interior illustrations copyright © 2004 by Lesley Harker. Cover illustration copyright © 2009 by C.B. Canga.

All rights reserved. Published in the United States by Random House Children's Books, a division of Random House, Inc., New York. Originally published in Great Britain as *The Starburster* by Young Corgi Books, an imprint of Random House Children's Books, London, in 2004.

Random House and the colophon are registered trademarks and A Stepping Stone Book and the colophon are trademarks of Random House, Inc.

Visit us on the Web!
www.steppingstonesbooks.com
www.randomhouse.com/kids

Educators and librarians, for a variety of teaching tools, visit us at
www.randomhouse.com/teachers

Library of Congress Cataloging-in-Publication Data
Doherty, Berlie.
[Starburster]
The goblin baby / by Berlie Doherty ; illustrated by Lesley Harker.
  p. cm.
Originally published in Great Britain under title: The starburster. London :
Random House Children's Books, 2004.
"A Stepping Stone book."
Summary: After nine-year-old Tam's baby sister is stolen away by faeries and replaced by a goblin baby, he must journey to the land of the faeries to retrieve her and bring her back home.
ISBN 978-0-375-85841-3 (pbk.) — ISBN 978-0-375-95841-0 (lib. bdg.)
[1. Fairy tales. 2. Changelings—Fiction. 3. Fairies—Fiction.] I. Harker, Lesley, ill.
II. Title.
PZ8.D6665Go 2009
[Fic]—dc22   2008037097

Printed in the United States of America

10 9 8 7 6 5 4 3 2   First American Edition

Contents

Blue   1

Sapphire Stars   8

The Changeling   13

Pixilated   18

"Only You Can Do It, Tam"   23

Something of Silver and
    Something of Velvet   29

Through the Green Passage   35

Prince Tamlin   39

Go Wisely, Go Bravely   47

The Sapphire Lake   50

The Fairy Castle   57

The Food of Fairies   64

The Starburster Is Stolen   71

Tanta   75

The Baby Glade   82

Keekwee Baba   87

The Secret Tower   91

Blue Is Found   96

The King of the Fairies   101

The Starburster   107

Home   113

Blue

On the day Tam's baby sister was born, he painted his finger blue.

"Look at that boy with the blue finger," some people said. "He must be very special."

One of these people was his great-grandpa Toby. He winked at Tam and said, "You must be very special. Your little sister will be proud of you one day."

Other people said, "Look at that boy with the blue finger. He must be very silly."

One of these people was Dad. "Don't be silly, Tam," he said. "You don't want your little sister to be scared of you, do you?"

He made Tam wash the paint off and took him to the hospital to see Mum and the baby. Mum was in bed and the baby cried all the time, and Tam wished he still had his blue finger.

On the day the baby was brought home from the hospital, Tam hid in the bathroom. The baby cried all the time when she wasn't drinking milk from Mum. Tam decided to make her a drink of her own. He squeezed some toothpaste into a glass of warm water and stirred it round with the end of his toothbrush, then carried it carefully downstairs.

"My word, she'll enjoy that," Great-grandpa Toby said.

But Dad took one sniff and poured it down the sink.

"Would you like to hold Baby for a bit?" Mum asked.

"No," said Tam, and ran up to his room. "I wish that baby would go away!" he shouted.

Great-grandpa followed him. "I've got a present for you, Tam," he said. "It's my most special thing." He went into his room and came back with a yellow sock in his hand.

"A sock?" said Tam.

"Look inside it," Great-grandpa said.

Tam put his hand in the sock and pulled out a little tube.

"Hold it up to your eye and swirl it round," said Great-grandpa. "What do you see?"

It was the most marvelous thing. When Tam looked through it, he could see eight Great-grandpas all cut into little pieces. He couldn't stop giggling. When he turned it toward the bed, he could see eight beds all topsy-turvy, and all kinds of patterns of colors. He had eight new red robes, and they swayed and billowed like princes' cloaks. And when he looked out the

window, he could see eight gardens in tiny slices of color, as brilliant as rainbows.

"It's called a kaleidoscope," said Great-grandpa. "But I call it a starburster. Yes, starburster's a good name for it."

"Can I really keep it?" Tam asked. He couldn't stop looking at things and twisting the tube round to make them glow and splinter and swirl with colors. It really did look as if stars were bursting open inside it.

"Of course you can. Shall we go down and look at Baby through it?"

Baby was asleep when they went down-stairs. Tam looked through the kaleidoscope at her and twisted it this way and that, so there were eight pink blobs and sixteen fisty hands and sixteen stubby feet.

"Would you like to hold her?" Dad said.

"No thank you," said Tam, peering at

him through the kaleidoscope. "You've broken into lots of pieces."

"What shall we call her?" Mum asked.

"Your faces are like balloons," Tam giggled, peering at Mum. "And all your noses are all over the place."

"My word, I bet you'd look funny holding the baby," Great-grandpa said. "Can I have a look?"

So Tam gave Great-grandpa the starburster and sat next to Mum on the couch, and Mum put the baby into his arms. Tam couldn't believe how soft she was, and how light and warm and sweet-smelling, and how quiet and still and gentle, and how peaceful her breathing was. Her hands fluttered open like butterflies and her fingers wrapped themselves round his thumb. Tam didn't dare move in case he dropped her. He hardly dared breathe. Then, for a second, her eyes opened. They were as blue as the sky. She stared right at Tam.

"What do you think of her?" Mum asked.

"I love her." Tam's voice was just a whisper. "Can we call her Blue?"

Sapphire Stars

When Tam wasn't cuddling Blue, he was playing with his starburster. He looked at everything through it, and everything looked strange and wonderful. But the best thing of all was looking at the stars. They shone and sparkled and danced through the starburster as though they were birds made of diamonds. Dad had to keep coming up to Tam's room and putting the starburster back in its yellow sock so Tam would go to sleep.

"I don't know which I love best," Tam said, "my starburster or Blue."

Then, one night, something awful happened. Blue was stolen.

The night started off very well. Tam was looking through his starburster, and he noticed that some of the stars seemed to be swarming like bees. They seemed to be coming toward the house. They seemed to be brilliant blue.

He shouted to Great-grandpa, who woke up at once and came hurrying into Tam's room.

"My word, they're like sapphires," Great-grandpa said, twisting the kaleidoscope excitedly.

"What's a sapphire?" Tam asked.

"It's a precious stone. It's very rare. A jewel. And it's blue."

"But why have the stars turned into sapphires?" Tam asked.

"My word, I don't know everything!" Great-grandpa said. "Better go to sleep now, Tam."

And Tam did try to go to sleep, but a strange sound kept waking him up. It was like the sound of tiny wings beating, like hundreds of moths fluttering against the window.

At last he drifted off to sleep, and in no time at all he was woken up by the sound of Blue crying. Then the crying turned to screaming. He put his fingers in his ears and tried to block the noise out. "That's the trouble with babies," he said to himself. "They never stop crying."

The screaming turned to a wailing that was so high-pitched he thought his ears would break. It was the worst sound Blue had ever made. In fact, it didn't sound like Blue at all. Mum was shouting now, and Dad was shouting, and then Mum started crying, too. Then the high-pitched sound turned into a howl like a dog, and Tam sat up and jumped out of bed. What *was* the matter with her? The howling suddenly turned into shrieks of laughing. But Blue never laughed like that. She was far too young yet to do anything but gurgle and chuckle.

Tam ran into Blue's room. They were all in there—Mum, Dad, and Great-grandpa—all gathered round the baby's crib and staring into it. No one was making any attempt to pick her up.

"Blue, Blue, what's the matter?" Tam shouted. He ran to the crib and stared down at the ugliest baby he had ever seen. It had pointed ears and a tippety nose and a screwed-up, cross little face.

"What happened?" Tam asked. "Where's Blue?"

Mum burst into tears. "Blue's been stolen," she sobbed. "And this little goblin thing's been left in her place."

The Changeling

Tam couldn't take his eyes off the goblin thing. It really was very ugly. But its eyes were as brilliant as blue jewels.

"Sapphires," Tam whispered to Great-grandpa. "Just like those stars we saw."

"What did you say?" Dad asked.

Great-grandpa looked worried.

"The stars were whizzing about last night, weren't they, Great-grandpa? They were deep, deep blue, just like her eyes," said Tam. "And things were flying and fluttering all round the house."

Dad sat down with his head in his hands.

"Why didn't you tell me? You silly old man!"

"You were asleep," Great-grandpa Toby muttered. "Anyway, it was nothing, it was nothing."

"What's all that got to do with this ugly thing in Blue's crib?" Mum demanded. "And where is Blue, anyway? Where's my baby?"

"Ask Grandpa," Dad said. "He reckons he knows about such things."

Great-grandpa took out his hankie and blew his nose loudly. "Yes, I think I do know. I think this baby is a changeling."

Mum gasped and started crying again.

Tam glared at the baby. She made a face at him and he made one back, his best one, with his eyes rolled up and his lips curled back like sausages. Instead of crying, the

baby giggled and tried to copy him.

"My word," said Great-grandpa, "I've never heard a little baby laugh like that before. It really must be a changeling."

"What's a changeling?" Tam asked.

"A changeling is a fairy child," said Great-grandpa.

"I've heard of this happening," Mum sobbed. "The fairies come and steal a mortal baby and leave a nasty little gobliny thing in its place. I'll never see my baby again!"

The changeling baby stopped making faces at Tam and smiled sweetly at him instead. She held out her arms as if she wanted him to pick her up.

"She's really, really ugly," said Tam.

Mum burst into tears again and ran out of the room, and Dad ran after her. Great-grandpa sighed deeply and sat on the chair. The changeling baby gurgled up at Tam.

"She likes you," Great-grandpa said.

"Well, I don't like her. I'd rather have Blue back, any day." Tam tried not to catch the goblin-thing's eyes, but she was smiling her crooked smile and staring straight at him with her dazzling blue eyes. It made him feel very strange. He could hardly take his eyes off her.

"She's bewitching you," Great-grandpa said.

"No, she's not," said Tam. "I'm not going to look at her."

But as soon as he said it, he wanted to look at her again. He went to bed, but all he wanted to do then was to go back to the changeling's room and peer round the door at her. Maybe what Great-grandpa had said was true. Maybe she *had* bewitched him.

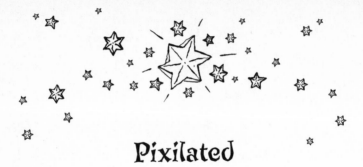

Pixilated

Mum and Dad refused to go near the changeling, but Tam was worried that she might be hungry. He took her some corn-flakes and she scowled at him. He took her a bottle of milk and she crossed her eyes.

"She seems all right," Great-grandpa said. "And I don't suppose she'd eat mortal food, anyway."

When no one was looking except Tam, the baby stared at a vase of roses till all the flowers flew across

the room and landed in her crib. She gobbled them up greedily, thorns and all. Then she lay back, burping loudly.

"Can I carry her into the garden?" Tam asked Mum. "I think she likes flowers."

"Just leave her alone," Mum said. "Try to forget she's here."

But how could they forget? The changeling shrieked and howled whenever Tam wasn't in her room. As soon as he went in, she stopped. They played the faces game for hours.

"My word, better not go out when the wind's blowing," Great-grandpa said.

"Soon as it stops, your face will stick like that."

"It's not my fault," said Tam. "She's making me do it. It's her eyes."

She could do other things with her eyes. She could make all kinds of things happen. When she stared at the cupboard, the doors flew open and all the things in it tumbled out in a mess on the floor. Then she just chuckled and closed her eyes and went to sleep, and nobody but Tam knew it had anything to do with her.

"Did you make that mess?" Mum demanded.

"No, it was the baby," Tam said.

"Don't be silly. Babies can't climb out of their cribs and open doors," Mum said. "Not even gobliny things like this one." But she glared at the sleeping baby all the same.

If the baby stared at the clock, the cuckoo

popped in and out of its door so wildly that it drove everybody mad with its cuckooing. Nobody saw her do it except Tam.

CUCKOO!

In the end Dad took the clock off the wall and put it in the garbage can. They could hear it cuckooing to itself out in the yard.

"*Cuckoo,*" sang the goblin baby. "*Cuckoo.*"

"Be quiet!" shouted Mum.

The baby stared at the window and the glass shattered like stars.

"My word, this house is pixilated all right," Great-grandpa chuckled. "I haven't had such fun in years."

"What's *pixilated*?" Tam asked.

"Bewitched, enchanted, full of mischief," Dad said.

Tam leaned over the baby's crib, and she blew bubbles at him.

"It's you, isn't it?" Tam whispered. "Pixilating everything, that's what you're doing. I think we should call you Pix."

And the baby smiled at him so sweetly that he actually smiled back. He just couldn't help it.

Great-grandpa came and stood next to him. "My word, you mustn't let her charm you," he said. "Your poor mum's very upset. That baby has to go."

"Go where?" Tam asked.

"Where she belongs," whispered Greatgrandpa. "Faery, that's where she comes from. The land of the fairies. Someone's got to take her back there, Tam."

"Only You Can Do It, Tam"

As soon as Mum and Dad had gone out of the room, he said it again, only louder, so Tam couldn't pretend he hadn't heard him.

"Someone has to take her to Faery, give her back to the king of the fairies, find Blue, and bring her home."

"I suppose so," Tam agreed.

"And only you can do it, Tam. My word, you're a brave boy."

"Me? But I can't do that! I'm only nine years old!" Tam said.

"Exactly," Great-grandpa Toby agreed. "That's why you have to do it."

"But I don't even know how to get there."

"I know the way in," Great-grandpa said. "It's called the green passage."

"How do you know that?"

"Because I once met someone who'd actually been there! He was a very old man, but when he went in, he was just a little boy, like you. And when he came out, he was an old, old man with a beard down to his toes. He'd been there a hundred years, and it just seemed like a day, he said."

"Great-grandpa, I'm not going."

"He told me how to get there, if I ever wanted to go. I never dared. I wasn't brave enough. But I used to go and sit by the green passage and wait in case any fairies came out. I thought I saw the king of the fairies himself at that very spot, when I was looking through my starburster. Just for a second, I thought I saw him, all dressed in green, with hair like dandelion fluff. I think he wanted my starburster, but he wasn't going to get it. That was ninety years ago." He opened his eyes wide with surprise. "Ninety years!"

"I don't want to go, Great-grandpa."

"You have to take something of your own that's silver and something of your own that's velvet, or you'll never get past the guardian. That's what the old man told me."

Tam sighed with relief. "Well, I can't do it. I haven't got anything of silver, and I haven't got anything of velvet."

Great-grandpa shook his head. "I think you have, Tam. I'm sure you have. And you have to give your favorite thing of all to the king of the fairies."

"My favorite thing? That's not fair!"

"If he gives you Blue back, that's fair, isn't it?"

Tam nodded sadly. He'd almost forgotten about Blue, he'd gotten so used to Pix.

"You have a think, and I'll have a nap," said Great-grandpa. He yawned noisily. "There's something else you have to do, only I can't remember what it is. If you don't do it, you won't come back for a hundred years, like that old man I met. Only I can't remember what it is." He went off to his own room to lie down.

"I really don't want to go!" Tam called after him.

Pix was making her favorite high-pitched yelping noises. The moon was shining into her crib and she was holding out her hands as if she was trying to pull herself up onto its

beams. Tam went to his own bedroom. Mum and Dad would be trying to sleep, he knew, but Pix would be keeping them awake, like she always did. He tried to sleep himself, but it was impossible. Her screeches were getting louder. He went back to her room and put his hand through the bars of her crib, and she grabbed hold of his fingers.

"What's the matter, Pix?" he asked. "Do you want to go home?"

As soon as he said that, she stopped crying. And right away she fell asleep, smiling.

Great-grandpa hurried into the room with his felt slippers flapping and his eyes shining. "I've just remembered what that other thing was! If you don't want to stay in Faery for a hundred years, you have to get there before the stroke of noon on mid-summer's day. That's tomorrow, Tam!"

Something of Silver
and Something of Velvet

Tam didn't sleep a wink that night. He lifted
Pix out of her crib and carried her into his
room and put her on his bed. Then he
searched through his toys to see if he had
something of silver
and something of
velvet to take. He
knew what his fa-
vorite thing was,
of course. He had
no doubt about
that, but he wasn't

at all happy about giving it to the king of the fairies.

Great-grandpa fussed round the room, clapping his hands and saying, "My word, I can't believe it! Young Tam's going to Faery!"

Tam sat back on his heels. "I don't want to go. But I'm going to rescue Blue," he said, trying to make himself feel brave and happy about it.

"Something velvet and something silver," Great-grandpa reminded him. "Be quick. Oh, I've remembered something else! The silver thing has to be sharp."

"Something silver and sharp," Tam said, gazing at his pile of things. "Like a . . ."

"Sword!" they both said together, and Pix woke up and stared at the closet, and out fell Tam's toy sword. She closed her eyes and chuckled.

"But it isn't sharp at all, because it's only plastic," Tam said. "And it isn't really silver. It's only gray paint."

"Never mind," said Great-grandpa. "It'll do. Something velvet now."

They looked hopelessly round the room.

"Cotton curtains," muttered Great-grandpa. "They're no use. Anyway, they're  your mum's. It has to be something of yours."

They stared at the window. Dawn was coming. If they didn't find something soon, it would be too late. Pix started crying, opened her eyes again, and glared at the door. And there it was. It just flew off the hook where it always

hung and draped itself round Tam's shoulders.

"My red robe!" he said. "With its velvet collar!" He stroked the collar. How he loved the feel of it, rough one way, smooth the other, just like a cat's nose.

Great-grandpa took it off Tam's shoulders and rolled it up. He carried it downstairs and put it at the bottom of Pix's carriage, then he came back up for Pix and carried her down. Tam followed with the sword and put it carefully in the carriage across Pix's blankets. He couldn't help feeling a surge of excitement as he laid it there. His hand stretched across to touch the sword.

"Use it carefully," Great-grandpa Toby warned.

"Use it?" said Tam, suddenly scared. "How do I use it?"

"I'm sure the guardian will give you instructions," Great-grandpa said. "There are bound to be Faery rules. They can't just let anyone wander round and do what they like there, can they? Now, Tam, fetch the favorite thing."

Pix chuckled gleefully.

"I wish I didn't have to," said Tam.

"I know," said Great-grandpa.

Tam went back to his room and opened the drawer by the bed. He took out the starburster in its yellow sock. He had a lump in his throat. He felt sadder than he had ever felt before. He carried it downstairs and put it in the carriage without saying anything, and Great-grandpa didn't say anything, either.

But an amazing thing happened then. The changeling baby stretched out her hands as if she wanted to touch it. Then she nodded her head and smiled, as if she understood exactly what was going on.

Through the Green Passage

They left the house just as the sun was pushing above the rooftops. All the air seemed to be golden that morning. They didn't wake Mum and Dad, though Tam was longing to tell them that he was going to find Baby Blue and bring her home again. But he knew Mum would worry and fuss and cry, and that would never do. Tam would never be able to leave if she did that. And Dad would insist on coming with him, and that would never do, either. Dad wasn't a little boy.

So he and Great-grandpa and Pix in her

carriage went out of the house as quietly as they could, down the street and through the park and across the river and toward the boulders. At last Great-grandpa stopped.

"This is the place. This is where I met the man with the long white beard that came to his toes."

"But it's just a pile of rocks," Tam said. "This can't be Faery."

Pix was growling and grunting, waving

her hands about and kicking her feet in the air, rocking the carriage so wildly that Tam thought she would fall out of it at any minute.

"See that crack between those big pointed rocks?" said Great-grandpa.

Tam nodded.

"That's the green passage. You have to go through there." He bent down and kissed Tam. "My word, you're a brave boy."

Tam's courage was draining away. He didn't feel a bit brave. He wanted to go back home and have a nice breakfast of toast and marmalade instead of going to Faery.

"I don't really want to . . . ," he began.

"I'm proud of you," Great-grandpa said.

So Tam gripped the handle of Pix's carriage and walked toward the crack. He turned round, and Great-grandpa nodded and waved and blew him a kiss. He turned back, and the two great boulders began to roll apart, and the narrow crack opened out to a passage that was as green as summer leaves. Tam took two more steps, then three, then seven, and he was inside the passage. He took two more, and the two great boulders rolled together again like huge doors closing behind him.

Prince Tamlin

It was completely dark now, and completely silent. Tam stood very still, and he and Pix both held their breath.

Something was happening. Tam could hear the sound of shuffling feet, and they were getting closer, closer. They stopped in front of Pix's carriage. Now Tam could hear the sound of someone breathing.

Suddenly there was a flash like blue lightning and the passage was lit by a flickering light. Standing in front of Tam was a skinny old man with a green beard and long green hair. He stared at Tam, and Tam stared back at him, too afraid to speak.

The old man pointed a bony finger at him and said, "Splix."

"Splix?" Tam said back.

"Who? Splix! Who?" the man asked, stamping his foot.

"Who? Tam, I'm Tam. Are you . . . are you the king of the fairies?"

"Sploof!" the skinny man growled. "Not king! Look-after. I look after."

"Oh! Are you a sort of guardian?" Tam asked the man.

"All of 'em's look-after." The skinny man swung his arms, and the floor of the passage lit up. Men were lying all around them, as still as stones.

"Faery soldiers," he whispered.

"Are they all dead?" Tam asked.

"Sploof!" the old man said again. "Slumber. Hinx hundert year-in, year-out." He held up ten fingers.

"Ten hundred! They've been asleep for ten hundred years. A thousand years?"

Look-after grinned, showing pointed green teeth.

"Can't they ever wake up?" Tam asked.

At that moment Pix woke up from her own deep sleep and began to whimper, and at the sound of the baby crying, the sleeping soldiers turned over onto their backs.

"Whishht! Wheesh! Sheesh!" Look-after whispered. "Only wake when mortals make war on Faery."

"I'm not making war," Tam promised.

"I've just come to see the king of the fairies, and to bring Pix back, and to take Blue back home. Blue's my baby sister, and the fairies stole her, you see, but we want her back."

The guardian peered in the carriage. He and Pix made faces at each other. He put his hand in the carriage and rubbed his fingers up and down her back and nodded.

"Don't you like Faery baby?" he asked, puzzled.

Tam stared at Pix. He did like her, he realized. He liked her very much now. She didn't even look very ugly in the flickering green light of the cave.

"Yes, I do like her," he said. "But she's not my sister, you see."

The guardian frowned as if Tam's answer made no sense to him. "Don't want her?"

Tam sighed. "I want Blue," he whispered.

Look-after growled and made a face at

Pix, and she made one of her worst ones at him. Then his fingers stole toward the yellow sock, but Tam pulled it away from him.

"You can't have that," he said. "It's a present for the king of the fairies."

"King?" The guardian glared at Tam. He thrust his face up to him. "King far away."

"Great-grandpa says I'll need to take

Pix to the king himself." Tam was shaking now. "Please, will you help me?"

The guardian grunted and shook his head. "Only prince see king," he snapped. He walked round Tam, looking him up and down. "Snee snix?" he snarled.

"Snee snix?"

The man stamped his foot. "Snee snix? Sharp silver?"

"Oh yes." Trembling, Tam lifted his sword out of the carriage. "But I haven't come to make war with it. It's not sharp. It's only plastic really, and it's gray, not really silver."

But the guardian swished the sword this way and that, until it gleamed as bright as the moon in his hands. He gave it back to Tam. It was a real sword now, sharp and shining like ice, with a blue jewel set deep in the hilt.

"Snee snix splix?" he shouted. "Name him."

"Snee snix splix? Oh, what's the sword called?" Tam closed his eyes. He thought of the name of his street. "Winander," he said.

Look-after grunted. "Vinand'r, Vinand'r. Use Vinand'r well. When you see castle nightmares, snee snix, chop off heads with Vinand'r."

"Chop off their heads? I can't do that!" Tam said. "I can't chop off anyone's head!"

But the guardian just stamped his foot and hissed.

Tam put the sword back in the carriage. He tried to wrap it up, but the guardian whipped the robe out of his hands and shook it out. It turned into a cloak of deep-red velvet. He grunted with pleasure and swung it round Tam's shoulders, so it fell in soft folds round him. Tam felt magnificent.

The guardian placed the sword, Winander, in Tam's belt and stood back and grinned his green teeth at him.

"Prince Tamlin," he said, bowing his head. "Welcome to Faery."

Go Wisely, Go Bravely

A voice that was not Look-after's echoed round the passage. It came from the guardian's mouth, but it was deep and strong and frightening, not at all like his own crackly voice.

Nothing take from Faery, the voice said. *Nor food nor drink take, nor sleep in Faery have. Go wisely, go bravely, young prince.*

Tam looked round, but there was no one to be seen but the green-haired guardian and the sleeping figures.

"How will I find the king?" Tam asked. His voice was shaking a little.

Cross the sapphire lake.

"Sapphire!" Tam said. "Like the stars!"

Do not look at your reflection. You will fall into an enchanted sleep for thousands of years. Remember this . . . remember all these things. The voice was growing fainter.

"And then what do I do, when I've crossed the lake?" Tam asked. There was no answer. "And how do I get across it? And where is it, anyway?"

Silence, except for the echo of his own words. *Is it, anyway? Anyway? Way?*

The guardian was watching him, arms folded, head to one side, grinning his green toothy grin. "This way, that way," he chuntered in his crotchety old voice. "Kimble."

He clicked his fingers and ambled off, and Tam followed him. It was hard work, pushing the carriage over the stony ground, and he didn't want to risk waking the sleepers or making Pix cry. He followed the guardian as carefully as he could.

Now he could see daylight ahead of him, and the blue gleam of water. And on the shore of the sapphire lake, the old man with the green hair and green beard stopped, and disappeared, just like a candle flame that had been blown out.

The Sapphire Lake

Tam gazed across the lake, almost dazzled by its brilliance. It shimmered ahead of him as wide and as far as his eyes could see. There was no way round it or over it; no shore, no bridge. He felt like crying.

"Now what do I do?" he moaned.

Pix sat up in her carriage. "Wish, wish, a fairy wish," she whispered.

"Pix! Did you really say that? You can talk! You can sit up already! It's amazing!"

"Wish, wish, a fairy wish," she whispered again.

"All right. I wish we had a boat," Tam

said. And so it happened, just like that, all in a moment. The carriage rolled into the lake and bobbed there, big enough for two to sail in. Winander the sword became a mast, and Tam's red velvet cloak became a sail. As soon as Tam scrambled aboard, the

little boat began to skim across the water.

Pix squirmed in her carriage. "Stay still," Tam told her, and she gurgled rudely at him. She leaned over the side, pointing to the water and making faces at her reflection.

Tam stared ahead of him. He must not look into the lake. Whatever happened, he must not look.

Pix started shouting and waving her arms about. She could see something in the lake past her own reflection, something wonderful and beautiful that made her face light up with smiles. She twisted her head round to look at Tam, and her eyes were shining. She looked back over the side.

"Ooh, ooh," she crooned. She laughed and sang happily. "Oooh!"

Tam so much wanted to see what she could see. Surely he could look at the lake without seeing his own face in it. Ahead of him he could see only the brilliant glitter of blue light. If he wanted to see anything else, he must look over the side of the boat.

"Oh, oh, oh!" shouted Pix.

And all round Tam, hundreds of chattering voices whispered and sang, "Look and see, look and see. There is no such beauty in the mortal world. Look and see."

Tam couldn't resist it any longer. He had to look for himself. He leaned across to see what Pix could see, and at once she twisted round to him, frowning. He heard the voice that had come from the guardian in the green passage echoing round him:

Do not look at your reflection. You will fall into an enchanted sleep for thousands of years. Remember this. . . .

Tam pulled himself back quickly, and the whispering voices stopped.

Now the sky and the lake had turned a much deeper blue. It began to rain. The rain turned to hail and plinked into the bottom of the boat like little blue stones. Tam held out his hand and caught one in

his palm. It lay there, not melting but glimmering with fiery blue light.

"Fairy stones. They're jewels," he said. "They must be sapphires! I wish I could show Great-grandpa! He'd know what they are."

The sapphire was beautiful. It glinted and sparkled like a tiny piece of sky.

"Take it," the singing voices chanted. "Have it. It's yours."

"Mum would love this," Tam said to Pix. "I could take her one, just this one." He closed his fingers round the sapphire.

"Yours," the voices sang on. "Yours. Yours."

Pix scrambled round to face Tam, sending the boat-carriage rocking dangerously. Water slapped over the sides. She glared at him until shivers of fear ran up and down his spine.

And the guardian voice came again:

Nothing take from Faery. Nothing take from Faery.

Tam flung the jewel as far as he could into the lake. It splashed and sank, and sent out a ring of blue ripples that spread like a peacock's tail opening, wider and wider.

And out of the ripples rose a castle, gleaming white like snow, with golden turrets and towers, and crimson flags flying from its pinnacles.

The Fairy Castle

The little boat-carriage bumped against a shore of sparkling blue sand. Tam scrambled out and pulled the boat from the water. Pix gurgled and sang and kicked her legs and flapped her arms.

"All right, all right, don't be so *impatient*," Tam said. "You were just a tiny baby when we left home. You were tiny and helpless, and now look at you. What's happening, Pix?"

He put his cloak round his shoulders, fixed Winander back into his belt, slipped the yellow sock into his pocket, and then

bent down to lift Pix out of the carriage. She screeched and pointed at something behind him, and he turned round to see three beasts bearing down on him, snarl-

ing and howling. They had long heads like horses and fat bodies like bulldogs. They had claws like rusty nails. They had round red eyes like flames. They had teeth like twisted spikes and long yellow drip-

ping tongues. One was red, one was black, and one was white. And they thundered toward the shore.

"Pix frightened," she whimpered.

"I am a bit scared

myself." Tam looked round desperately for somewhere to hide, but there was nowhere.

Pix whimpered again.

When you see castle nightmares, snee snix, came the voice of the guardian.

Tam felt the hilt of the fairy sword against his hand. He drew it out of his belt and swung it round in the air.

Snee snix, chop off heads with Vinand'r.

Wheesh! Wheesh! Winander sang. The nightmare beasts reared up toward Tam. He closed his eyes and gripped the hilt tightly. *Wheesh! Wheesh! Wheesh!* He chopped off their heads.

Tam opened his eyes and saw the three heads rolling into the lake. The black beast turned into a girl with black hair, the red beast turned into a girl with red hair, and the white beast turned into a girl with white hair. They danced round Tam.

"Thank you, thank you!" they said. "We're free! We're free!"

Tam put Winander back into his belt. He was shaking.

"What happened?" he asked. "How did you do that?"

The girl with black hair laughed. "You did it! You broke the king's spell. You set us free."

"We're fairies again," the red-haired girl sang. They opened wings like dragonflies', green and blue and gold, and skimmed round Tam, talking one after the other in a dizzying jumble.

"But why did the king turn you into nightmares?" Tam asked. "How could he be so cruel?"

The fairy girls all spoke at once again.

"He sent us to mortal land . . ."

"Long ago . . ."

"To find what he most desired."

"But we couldn't find it . . ."

"And when we came back without it . . ."

"He was so angry with us . . ."

"That he turned us into nightmares."

"He said only a brave young prince . . ."

"From the land of mortals . . ."

"Could break the spell."

"And that was you," they finished, smiling.

"But I'm only Tam," Tam said.

"Prince Tamlin," Pix reminded him. She flapped her arms like the three fairies, then lost her balance and tumbled backward. She stuck her thumb in her mouth and scowled.

"And now we're free!" the girls laughed. "Thank you, Prince Tamlin!" They darted away from him, over the sapphire lake. The sound of their laughter floated away like bells.

"I wonder what it was he told them to find?" Tam said. "The king must be very, very cruel to turn them into nightmares like that. I hope he doesn't do the same to me, Pix. But I'll have to risk it, all the same. I wonder if he's in there."

He looked up toward the castle. He could see figures on the parapets and leaning out of the towers. Three trumpets were raised—a bronze trumpet, a silver trumpet, and a golden trumpet—and they played a sweet fanfare of welcome that sounded like a forest of birdsong.

Pix raised her arms up to Tam. "Take Pix home."

The Food of Fairies

Sandy-colored children ran toward Tam and Pix and led them over six stepping stones and through the castle doorway into a courtyard. In the middle was a fountain that showered a plume of stars. The stars drifted down into a pool of silver water. And there were flowers everywhere — trees filled with flowers, arches of flowers, lawns of flowers. The children ran here and there as if they were showing Pix and Tam how beautiful it all was.

"Home! Home!" Pix struggled to be out of Tam's arms, and he set her down gladly.

She seemed to be growing heavier and bigger by the minute. And he had noticed something strange about her back. Her shoulder blades seemed to be pushing out through the little spotted nightgown that used to belong to Blue. And when she looked up at him, her face was different. She'd lost that hairy, scowly look that she used to have.

She tried to stand up, clinging on to his leg for support, but bumped back down again. She flapped her arms and grumbled. Then she reached out to an archway of roses and clung on to that.

Flower petals showered round her, and she grabbed them by the fistful and stuffed them in her mouth.

"Be careful," Tam warned her. "They might be full of grubs."

Pix burped and grinned up at him. Petals were stuck to her wet cheeks and her chin and clung to her hair. She held out a fistful to him and he shook his head.

Then Tam noticed that the other children were eating flowers, too, only more daintily than Pix. They wandered from flower to flower, picking a white petal here and a pink one there and smiling as if they tasted wonderful. It made his stomach growl to watch them. A girl with deep purple eyes ran over to him, holding out a wooden bowl full of petals.

"Welcome!" she said. "Are you hungry? Nectarine flowers, orange blossom, cherry blossom. Eat, Prince Tamlin." She shook the bowl, and the petals turned into gossamer

froth that looked like cotton candy and smelled as sweet as strawberries.

A boy came with a crystal goblet of petals, and when he shook it, the petals turned into a sparkling liquid like lemonade. He held it out to Tam, nodding at him to take it. Tam was so hungry now that he felt weak. His throat was dry with thirst. The first girl dipped a chocolate twig into the bowl and put it to his lips. Tam closed his mouth firmly and shook his head.

"Mustn't!" he said, but *oh!* he was dizzy with hunger.

The children clustered round him with their bowls of delicious-smelling petals. "Just one, just one," they whispered. The purple-eyed girl held out the chocolaty twig again, and it was so close to his face that he could almost taste the smell. He covered his mouth with his hand, and a voice from nowhere boomed out:

Nor food nor drink take.

Startled, the children sprang away from Tam, looking this way and that to see where the voice was coming from.

"He can see us!" the purple-eyed girl said. "He knows!"

"Who?" Tam asked. "Is it the king?"

And as if he had said the most frightening word that could be imagined, the children dropped their bowls and petals and covered their faces with their hands. And the strange thing was, Tam's hunger and thirst had completely gone.

He turned round to look for Pix and saw that she had curled up on the grass and fallen asleep. Some of the other children were sleeping, too, or yawning, or rubbing their eyes.

The air was hot and sweet with the scent of flowers. Tam could hardly keep his eyes open. He was drowsy with the dazzle of sunlight and flowers, and all round him he could hear the steady breathing of sleeping children as one after another they sank to their knees and curled up on the grass. He yawned, and yawned again. "Mustn't sleep, must stay awake," he yawned. His head was so muzzy that he couldn't remember anymore why he had to stay awake.

Two of the children came to him and took his hands. They led him to a hammock made of flowers and stitched with daisy chains. He allowed himself to be lifted onto it and rocked gently, backward and forward, backward and forward. "Sleep, Prince Tamlin. Sleep," they sang, and their voices were so soft and sweet that all he wanted to do was to close his eyes, close his eyes, close his . . . close . . . cl . . .

The Starburster Is Stolen

"No! I mustn't!"

He opened his eyes as wide as he could and stared round.

Nor sleep in Faery have.

"No, I didn't, I wasn't, I wouldn't," Tam stuttered.

But he was the only one to hear the voice this time. All the children were awake now, playing a game of some kind, throwing something in the air, laughing and squealing. Pix was running across the grass toward him, shouting to him to come.

"Look, Prince Tamlin, look!" she called.

The girl with purple eyes laughed across at Tam and threw something. She caught the thing that they were playing with and threw it up in the air again. Now Tam could see something yellow slipping away and falling to the ground. The tube that was inside gleamed as it rose out of her hands.

"Hey! That's my starburster!" shouted Tam. He struggled out of the hammock and ran to a golden-haired boy who had caught the starburster, but as soon as Tam reached him, the boy opened his wings and skimmed away. He passed it to another child, who passed it to another.

Tam ran helplessly from one to the other, jumping and skipping to try to keep up. The purple-eyed girl caught it just as he reached her. She flew up above his head, tossing the kaleidoscope from one hand to the other like a juggling stick,

teasing him. Then she flew to a tree by
the pool and hung upside down from one
of the branches. She dangled there, just
out of his reach.

"Please give it back to me!" begged Tam. "I must have it. It's a present for the king of the fairies."

A hush of wonder fell over the children.

"The king!" the girl in the tree gasped. "You're going to see the king!"

"Some fairies stole my baby sister and left Pix instead," Tam said. "So I've brought Pix back, and now I want Blue. And Great-grandpa said I have to give the starburster to the king. Please, please give it back to me."

"You must be very brave, if you're going to see the king," one of the boys said. "Give him his starburster, Elfa."

"Here," Elfa said. "Take it." She let the kaleidoscope slip out of her fingers, but it caught on one of the branches and bounced off as Tam ran to catch it. It fell into the pool with a splash of rainbow light and sank to the bottom, out of sight.

Tanta

Tam stared at the pool. He couldn't believe what had happened. Pix put her hand in his and let out a howl of rage.

"What's happening out here?" A woman came running toward them, her golden hair and yellow gown billowing round her.

"Tanta! Tanta's coming!" Elfa flew down from her tree and ran to join the other children. They stood holding hands, quiet and still. One of the boys made a bubbling noise, as if he were trying to keep his giggles inside himself.

The woman stopped and looked down

at Tam. Her hair was as bright as sunshine round her face, and her eyes were like silver moons. Tam thought she was more beautiful than anyone he had ever seen.

"Are you the queen of the fairies?" he asked.

The children squawked and giggled, and the woman glared at them until they fell silent again. Then she turned back to Tam.

"I am not the queen of the fairies," she said. "I am Tanta! And who are you?"

"Tam," he whispered, all his courage gone.

"Prince Tamlin," Pix mumbled. She gripped his hand tightly.

Tanta looked down at Pix and plucked at her grubby nightgown. She turned her round and felt her knobbly shoulder blades. "I've never seen you before. You don't belong here."

"I do! I do!" Pix sobbed. She held out her arms to Tam and he picked her up. She put her arms round his neck and he hugged

her tightly. His throat hurt so much that he could hardly speak.

"I've come all this way to bring Pix back," he said. "I walked through the green passage and I didn't wake the sleepers up. I sailed across the sapphire lake and I didn't take anything. I didn't look at my face in the water. I chopped off the nightmares' heads and turned them back into fairies. I didn't eat when I was hungry. I didn't drink when I was thirsty. I didn't fall asleep when I was tired. I did all that so I could bring Pix here and so I could find my  baby sister and take her back to Mum. But I have to give my favorite thing to the king, and I haven't got it anymore."

Tanta stood with her arms folded, nodding her head. "I believe you," she said. "You look like a brave boy who could do all of that. And what is this favorite thing that you were going to give to the king of the fairies?"

"It's my starburster. It's like magic but it isn't really, Great-grandpa says. It's just clever and beautiful." Tam swallowed hard. "And it's gone."

"Gone where?"

Tam couldn't say any more. It was all too much. He stared at the pool and tears trickled down his cheeks. The fairy children gasped in horror and clustered round him, stroking his cheeks, patting him, whispering, "Don't break, Prince Tamlin. Don't break."

"Now stop that," said Tanta. "It's too sad."

Then she did an amazing thing. She stood on the edge of the pool and dived into it, and as she dived she turned into a golden fish. Seconds later she came up out of the pool in a ring of ripples and leaped into the air like a salmon. She twisted round and became herself again, standing next to

Tam, completely dry. She held the star-burster in her hands.

"Can I look?" she asked.

Tam nodded. He was too surprised to speak. He had actually seen fairy magic. *Wait till I tell Great-grandpa!* he thought.

Tanta lifted up the kaleidoscope and peered through it. She twisted it this way and that, peering at the water and the fountain and the sky and the flowers, and it seemed as if she never wanted to stop looking through it. "Man magic!" she said softly. "How wonderful it is."

She gave it back to Tam at last and watched how carefully he snuggled it into the yellow sock. He put it into his pocket and kept his hand over it, just in case.

"Come with me to the baby glade," Tanta said. "We'll see if we can find your sister."

The Baby Glade

Tanta led Tam and Pix to a shady orchard. Dabs of sunlight filtered through the leaves of fruit trees. In the cool shadows cradles were being rocked by tall elves. They all looked alike, with pointed ears and green eyes and flowing white hair.

Most of the babies were sleeping. Some were holding their hands up toward the trees, as if they wanted to catch the dapples of sunlight and shadow. Some were playing with their toes. They made the little gurgling sounds that Pix loved to make. Some bigger babies were sitting on the

grass, picking tiny flowers and sucking the petals. From time to time they flapped their arms up and down.

A very few of them had tiny buds of feathers sprouting from their shoulder blades. And there were about six who had fully grown wings that opened and shut,

opened and shut like the wings of butterflies. Pix pointed to them and waved
her arms up and down. They stood on the
tips of their toes and rose in the air, just
about leaving the ground, and landed
again with a bump. They laughed with
excitement.

"Very good, flightlings," Tanta said as she
passed them. "Soon you'll be flying. Then
you won't be in the baby glade anymore."

The flightlings smiled proudly at each
other.

"Why haven't you got wings?" Tam
asked Tanta shyly.

"Grown-ups don't have wings.
We don't need them. I lost mine
a long time ago."

"Don't you mind?" Tam
looked back to the children by
the fountain, swooping and

diving in the air like birds. How he would love to be able to do that.

"Mind?" Tanta put her head to one side and thought. "Nobody really minds growing up, Prince Tamlin. Though I must say, I loved my wings. They were golden. But as soon as I lost them, I was able to shape-change, and that's very useful."

"Is that how you turned into a fish? What else can you do?"

"That's my secret," Tanta said. "And I never, never shape-change unless it's really important. If I did it just for fun, the king would make me stay that shape forever."

"Like making faces? Great-grandpa says that if the wind changes when I'm making a face, I'll stay like that."

"Exactly. He sounds very wise, your great-grandpa. Now, have a look in the cradles and see if you can find your sister.

They don't have wing-buds when they're very small, so I really wouldn't know a fairy baby from a mortal baby."

"Mortal babies are prettier," Tam wanted to say, but didn't. He looked at Pix. She really was very pretty now that she was back in Faery. Even Mum would like her.

He went from cradle to cradle and peered inside every one. He didn't have to look for wing-buds to know that they were all fairies. Blue definitely wasn't there. When he came to the last cradle, he felt like crying again.

"Are there any more baby glades?" he pleaded. "She must be somewhere else."

Tanta shook her head. "All the babies are brought here as soon as they're born, and they stay with me till they can fly. I'm sorry, Prince Tamlin. There are no more babies in the whole of Faery."

Keekwee Baba

One of the elves had been holding Pix while Tam looked into the cradles. He came over now and said something in a strange language to Tanta.

"Keekwee baba?"

"Keekwee baba?" Tanta looked shocked. The elf pulled his ears and rocked his head from side to side.

Tanta turned back to Tam. "Morva says there is one more baby in Faery. But she's not your sister. She can't be."

Tam's heart rose. There was a chance; surely there was a chance. "Can I see her?"

"She's far away from here," Tanta said. "And she belongs to Keekwee. That's what the elves call the king and queen. You're not going to tell me that the queen would steal a human baby and bring her up as a fairy, are you?" She stood with her hands on her hips, glaring down at Tam. "If anyone even dared to suggest it, the king would turn them into tadpoles, or something much worse."

But Tam was already moving away. "Tell me where they live. I'm going to look."

"You'll never find your way there on your own," Tanta called after him. "They're in their secret tower. No one is allowed to go there unless they're sent for. Hardly anyone in Faery knows the way there. Even I don't."

The elf pulled his ears again and spoke in his quick, light voice. "Emba fost ni glaz pintos."

"Morva says it's over there, past the

emerald forest, up in the crystal mountains."
Tanta pointed to shimmering icy mountains
in the distance. "That's all he knows."

"I'll find it," said Tam. He took Pix out
of the elf's arms. "I'll get there."

"It's too far for you to walk, Prince Tamlin," Tanta insisted. "You're only a child."

"It doesn't matter. I'll get there, however
long it takes. I'm not going home without
Blue," Tam said. He was scared and
worried and excited, all at the same time.
"Come on, Pix."

He started off out of the baby glade
again, in the direction of the distant
crystal mountains. They seemed so far
away, and so high, and so icy,
that he had no idea how he
was going to do it. And
when he did get to the
secret tower, he had

the wicked king of the fairies to face.

"It seems so impossible," he whispered to Pix. "But we've got to do it."

And Pix whispered back, "Wish, wish, a fairy wish."

"A fairy wish!" sighed Tam. "How I wish a fairy would help me!"

Pix squirmed in his arms, pointing over his shoulder. Tam turned round and saw the most wonderful thing. Tanta had gone, and a horse was trotting toward them—a beautiful white horse with silver eyes like moons and a long, flowing golden mane.

"Tanta?" Tam said.

The horse stopped by him. "Yes," she said in a snorty, horsey voice.

The elf took Pix out of his arms, and Tam climbed onto Tanta's back. They set off, with Morva running in front of them, leading the way to the secret tower.

The Secret Tower

It was a long way. The emerald forest was deep and dark. The trees stretched out long fingers and pulled Tam forward and backward and sideways and nearly upside down. They plucked at his cloak, they scratched his cheeks, they pulled his hair. He could hear Pix whimpering with fright.

Morva held her up to Tam and he leaned down and took her. The little elf tumbled head over heels with relief. Pix was getting much too heavy to be carried.

Tam clicked his tongue. "On, on, Tanta," he urged. He rode with one arm round Pix and his free hand grasping Tanta's mane, while Morva ran ahead. It was better that way, and it was comforting for Tam to have Pix with him. She babbled happily into his

ear, chewing it from time to time.

When they came out of the emerald forest at last, the crystal mountains reared above them, shiny and smooth as glass, cold as ice. Morva took Pix for a while so Tam could rest his arms, then passed her back as they started to climb the mountain. Tanta's hooves slipped and slithered. Tam was jerked backward and forward, but he clung on to Pix and he hung on to the golden mane. He clicked his tongue.

"On, on, Tanta," he urged again.

And at last they could see the tower, as white as ice. Wispy clouds like veils swirled round it. Huge white birds with trailing feathers and piercing golden eyes swooped in and out of the mist.

"Keekwee tower!" Morva squatted on the ground with his legs crossed. He was trembling uncontrollably. He put his hands over his eyes as if he were trying to hide.

Tanta stopped. "I don't dare go any farther, Prince Tamlin," she said. "If the king sees me, he'll make me stay a horse forever. He might even turn me into a nightmare."

Tam slid down from her back, still clutching Pix, who was fast asleep. "Thank you for bringing me," he said. He couldn't take his eyes off the tower.

"Goodbye, Prince Tamlin. Good luck," Tanta said.

The last slope leading up to the tower was steep and slippery. Tam walked more and more slowly. He was shaking, but he didn't know whether it was with fear or tiredness. A flight of glass steps led up to the entrance, but he could hardly lift his legs to climb them. He gazed up at the tower in despair.

"I mustn't give up now, I mustn't give up now," he kept saying to himself. He put Pix down and she woke up immediately. She tried to stand up, wriggling her back from time to time as though her shoulders were itchy. There was a sudden tearing sound, and her grubby nightgown ripped in two places. The feathery tips of little wings poked through the holes.

"Pix! You're nearly a flightling!" Tam said.

"I know! I know!" She beamed up at him. "Can you see them? Can you see my wings?" Her tiny feathery wings opened up like daisies, then closed again.

But she still couldn't walk, and she still couldn't fly. Tam lifted her up again and staggered up the last few steps with her. He put her down by the amber door at the entrance to the tower.

"I can't carry you any farther," he panted. "You stay there and practice opening your wings. I'm going in on my own."

Blue Is Found

The inside of the tower was filled with golden light. Someone was singing a lullaby in a low, rich, beautiful voice that made Tam long to lie down and go to sleep.

"But I mustn't," he told himself. "I mustn't go to sleep. I must find Blue. I must find Blue."

The singing was coming from the center of the golden light. It nearly dazzled him, but he shielded his eyes with his hand and crept as close as he dared. And it was as if he were walking through a wall of light, because inside all the brightness everything

was dim and soft, like the glow of candles.
A woman with long dark hair the color of
plums was lying in a hammock made of
silvery spiderwebs. She wore a skirt of grass-
green silk and yellow satin shoes. She had

a sleeping baby in her arms and she was singing to it.

She seemed not to know that Tam was there. He tiptoed closer still, and closer. He was sure—he was so sure—that the baby was Blue.

The woman's singing grew fainter and slower. Tam could see that she was falling asleep. At last the singing stopped. The rocking stopped. The hammock stopped swinging. The fairy woman was fast asleep.

Tam took a deep, slow breath and stepped forward. One pace. Two paces. Three paces. So near, and now he could see the baby's face. It was. It was Blue.

Tam reached forward and touched the baby's cheek, very gently. She opened her eyes at once and stared at him with wonder. Then he put his hands under her and lifted her out of the fairy queen's arms.

"Stop!" A voice like thunder echoed round the tower. Sapphire-blue lights flashed around Tam. He clutched Blue close to him and tried to run through the outer ring of dazzling light toward the amber door. Now he could see that the blue lights were spiders, dipping and bobbing down toward him on silky strands. They danced round him, spinning their threads until they wrapped him so tightly that he couldn't move his arms or his legs.

And there in front of him, brighter than any light, was the king of the fairies. He was dressed in a long tunic of white linen. He had wild silver hair like a crown of dandelion fluff, and his eyes were golden and piercing. And he was furious. He raised both his fists above his head and strode toward Tam.

"How dare you come to Faery, mortal boy?" the king roared. "How dare you enter my secret tower? And how dare you steal my baby daughter?"

The King of the Fairies

Tam struggled helplessly in his gossamer bindings. If only he could get his right hand free, he could pull his sword Winander out of his belt and chop through the spider strands. But there was nothing he could do to free himself.

The queen was awake now. She came running to stand at the king's side. She stared at Tam.

"He's only a child," she said. "Don't bind him so tight."

The king snapped his fingers and the web bindings fell away from Tam as if they were strands of hair. The queen tried to take Blue out of Tam's arms, but he clung tightly to the baby. She snuffled and chuckled into his ear.

"Don't try to run away with her," the king said, "or I will turn you to stone forever." He smiled at the queen. "He would make a pretty statue for your rose garden."

"Who are you, and what are you doing here?" the queen asked Tam.

"And don't lie," the king said. "Fairies hate lies! I can read lies, and I can read the truth. If you lie, my spiders will bind you again." The spiders bobbed round Tam on their long threads. Their jewel eyes glistened.

"I'm Tam. The fairies call me Prince Tamlin." His voice was tiny and shaky, but as soon as he spoke, the spiders ate their threads and bobbed back up toward the hazy ceiling of the tower.

"Prince Tamlin," the king repeated with a mocking smile. "Well, you have your velvet cloak and your silver sword. I suppose you must be a prince. And what are you doing here, Prince Tamlin?"

Tam breathed deeply to find the courage to speak again. "You stole Blue away from us, but we want her back."

"How dare you accuse us of stealing!" the king roared.

"Fairies never steal," screamed the queen into Tam's face. "Fairies take what they want, but we always leave a gift behind."

"What we want, we always get," said the king. "Always. But our servants will have left you something in exchange." He stamped his foot. "We never steal."

Tam shouted back at him, "But you never

even asked us! You're wicked and cruel!" He closed his eyes. Now what had he done? "Why did you take our baby?" he whispered.

The queen stroked Blue's hand, and her voice became soft and sweet again. "I like mortal babies. My servants did well to choose this one. She will have a beautiful life here with us." She peered at Tam. "You could stay, too."

Tam shook his head fiercely. He was too scared to speak now. He looked up at the spiders, and they peered down at him with jet-black eyes. The king walked round and round him in silence.

"I can see he's a brave boy," he said at last. "But he won't do for Faery." He snapped his fingers in Tam's face. "Go away.

Go home. I won't punish you for coming. Leave the baby, and go home safely to the land of mortals."

"No," said Tam. He could feel Blue's soft breath against his cheek. "I came all this way. I came through the green passage without waking the sleepers up. I crossed the sapphire lake and I didn't look into it. I chopped off the heads of the nightmares. I did all these things so I could find Blue again and take her home. And I won't go home without her. I won't. I won't."

Again the queen tried to take Blue out of his arms, and again Blue and Tam clung to each other.

"I brought the fairy baby with me," Tam said. "She's called Pix. She can talk already. She's prettier than she used to be. She's very nice, but we didn't want her. We wanted our own baby. And I carried her most of the way here because she can't walk and she can't fly. She's very heavy, but I didn't drop her and I didn't leave her behind."

"And tell me," said the king suddenly, "how did you find my secret tower? How did you get here?"

Tam hesitated. The spiders began to bob down toward him again.

"I came through the emerald forest and over the crystal mountains," he said.

"On your own?" The king's golden eyes seemed to look right into Tam's mind.

Tam was cold with fear. If he lied, then the spiders would spin their threads round him again and he would never be free. He would never go home. But if he told the truth, Tanta and Morva would be punished. They would be turned into nightmares. He had no idea what to say.

The Starburster

"Whee! Look at Pix!" There was a sudden excited shout, and a bundle of feathers shot through the amber doorway and came hurtling into the tower. "Pix can fly!" she shouted, swooping round them, her starry wings spangling in the light. "Whee!"

The king and queen ducked as she whizzed over their heads. She skidded to a halt at their feet, stray feathers floating round her, and beamed up at Tam. She closed her wings and gasped for breath. "I'm a real fairy now!"

She fluttered her wings open and took

off again, just missing the king. The queen laughed and caught her.

"Not so fast!" she said. "You'll break your wings if you go as fast as that!"

Pix landed again.

"I'll show you," the queen said. She lifted her arms as if they were wings and moved them slowly and gracefully up and down. "Like this."

"This is Pix," Tam said. "Your servants left her behind in exchange for Blue. She can be your daughter."

"Yes, please!" said Pix. She smiled her best smile and fluttered her wings.

"She's very pretty," the queen said.

"And her wings are beautiful," the king said.

It was then that Tam knew that it was quite safe for him to put Blue down and rest his arms for a bit. Nobody was going to snatch her away. The king and queen were far too busy admiring Pix's starry wings. And just as he put Blue down in the hammock, Pix flew over to him and whispered, "Don't forget the special thing!" She whizzed away again, humming happily.

"The special thing! I nearly forgot!" Tam ran to the king. "I've brought you something in exchange for Blue! I've brought you a present," he said. He put his hand in his pocket and pulled out Great-grandpa's yellow sock.

"Thank you," said the king, not taking his eyes off Pix.

"It's not the sock," Tam explained. "It's what's inside it that's special."

"Thank you," the king said again. He

put his hand inside the sock and pulled out the kaleidoscope. His face lit up with surprise and pleasure. "I've seen one of these before!" he shouted. "Look! Look at my present! It's a . . . it's a . . ."

"It's a starburster," Tam said. "At least, that's what Great-grandpa calls it. You put it up to your eye and look through it."

"And you twist it this way, and you twist it that way," the king said. He held the starburster to his eye.

"The other end," Tam said, and turned it the right way round for him.

"Oh, man magic!" the king breathed, peering through the kaleidoscope. He danced on the tips of his toes with excitement. "Nothing in Faery is as wonderful as this. Oh, I've always wanted one of these." He walked round with it, peering at everything—at his feet, at the queen, at Pix's wings, at his spiders—and every new thing he looked at made him gasp and laugh out loud. "My word!" he said.

"That's what Great-grandpa says."

"I saw a little boy looking through one

of these once," the king said, still not taking the kaleidoscope away from his eye. "It was in the mortal land, and it was just outside the green passage. He was looking through a . . . a starburster just like this and he kept saying, 'My word! My word!' Oh, I so much wanted to see what he could see! I looked through the other end and he looked straight at me! And he shouted out loud, 'My word! A fairy!'"

Tam felt a great bubble of excitement inside him. "I know who it was! Was it about ninety years ago?"

"I think it was yesterday," the king said. He took the kaleidoscope away from his eye for just a second. "But time is different in Faery. Actually, Prince Tamlin, he looked a bit like you."

Home

The king and queen and Pix spent a long time looking through the kaleidoscope and laughing and exclaiming, "My word!" at every new thing they saw. Tam rocked Blue in the hammock, watching them. As soon as she woke up, he lifted her out and said, "If you don't mind, I think we'd better go now."

"Of course," said the king. He looked surprised, as if he had forgotten all about Tam. "I'll send for someone to show you the way. They'll be at the bottom of the glass steps."

"Thank you for bringing our fairy child back," said the queen. "Your sister is very nice, but I really think I like Pix better."

Pix flew up to Tam. She landed daintily and smiled up at him. "Goodbye, Prince Tamlin. Thank you for looking after me."

She fluttered her wings for him and Blue.

"It's all right, Pix," he said. His voice was husky. "Take care now." He couldn't bring himself to say goodbye, but walked slowly through the dazzling light and out through the amber archway.

And there, waiting for him at the bottom of the glass steps, were a white horse with a long, flowing golden mane and silver eyes, and an elf with green hair and pointed ears.

"Tanta and Morva! You're still here!" Tam ran down the steps. Morva helped him onto Tanta's back and handed Blue up to him. Then they were off, galloping like the wind, over the crystal mountains, through the emerald forest, and they came to the white castle.

"Off you get," said Tanta. "We can't take you any farther."

Tam handed Blue down to Morva and slid off Tanta's back, and when he turned round, the horse had gone, and there was golden-haired Tanta again, smiling at him and rocking Blue in her arms.

"Mortal babies are very beautiful!" she sighed. "No wonder the king and queen wanted one. And no wonder your mother wants her back. There's your boat, waiting for you."

Sure enough, there was the little boat-carriage on the blue sand. Morva helped Tam to push it into the water. He bowed to Tam and then clasped both of Tam's hands in his own.

"Far good, Tamlinkee," he said. "Far good, baba."

"Far good, Morva," said Tam. He climbed into the boat.

Tanta handed Blue down to Tam and

pushed the boat gently away from the shore. She clapped her hands.

"Goodbye, Prince Tamlin," she called. "Goodbye, Baby Blue."

The boat-carriage scudded across the sapphire lake with Winander for a mast and the velvet cloak for a sail, and in no time at all they had reached the other side. Tam pulled the boat out of the water and it became a carriage again.

"Nearly there, Baby Blue," he said, and

she gurgled sleepily at him. He trundled her over the rocky ground into the dark tunnel. A flickering light came toward him. Now he could see old Look-after, with his green hair and long green beard.

The elf came straight up to the carriage and peered inside. He grinned his green toothy grin and pointed a bony finger at Blue. She curled her own fingers round it and hiccuped.

"Splix?" Look-after asked.

"Splix? Oh, her name! She's called Blue. My baby sister, Blue," Tam said proudly.

"Baba satta, Blue," said Look-after softly.

Then he jerked his head and led Tam past the sleeping guardians to the dark cave. He bowed.

"Goodbye, Prince Tamlin!"

Tam paused for a mument. He could still hear Pix's voice, as clear as anything, laughing and singing far away. He could hear the queen and king of the fairies, he could hear Elfa and the other sandy-colored children, and Tanta and Morva, and then all the voices faded away.

Tam felt his cloak slipping away from his shoulders and Winander sliding out of his belt. He looked down and saw his robe and plastic toy sword on the stony ground and bent down to pick them up. And just as he put them at the bottom of Blue's carriage, two huge boulders at the end of the cave rolled apart, and daylight flooded through.

He pushed the carriage down the green passage. The boulders rolled in place behind him, and there sitting on the grass in front of him were Mum and Dad and Great-grandpa, eating sandwiches and drinking lemonade.

"My word," said Great-grandpa. "It's our Tam."

"Just in time for the picnic," said Dad.

And Tam lifted Blue out of the carriage and put her, safe and sound, into Mum's arms.